Spine-chilling True Ghost Stories of

FIRST RESPONDERS
EVE S EVANS

ALSO BY

EVES EVANS

Fiction:

The Haunting of Hartley House

Hartley House Homecoming

The Haunting of Crow House

The Haunting of Redburn Manor

Origins

Anthologies:

True Ghost Stories of First Responders

50 Terrifying Ghost Stories

Holiday Hauntings

Shadow People

Haunted Hotels

Haunted Hospitals

Haunted Objects

Paranormal Pets

The Ghosts Among Us

True Ghost Stories Haunted First Responders

For Del

Follow Eve and her books on Goodreads or Bookbub! And get notified of any new reads coming in 2022-2023.

The characters and events portrayed in this book are fictitious or are used fictitiously. Any similarity to real persons, living or dead, is purely coincidental and not intended by the author.

All brand names and product names used in this book are trademarks, registered trademarks, or trade names of their respective holders. The author and publisher are not associated with any product or vendor in this book.

All rights reserved. No part of this publication may be transmitted or reproduced in any form or by any means. This includes photocopying, electronic, mechanical, or by storage system (informational or otherwise), unless given written permission by the author.

Copyright © February 2022 Eve S Evans

FIREHOUSE APPARITIONS

I've resided next to a haunted firehouse for almost seventeen years. It's still in use today as a small holding station for fire engines and equipment, but it isn't in use 24/7 like the bigger stations in town. The firehouse itself is quite old-fashioned and somewhat run-down on the outside; ivy has begun to creep along one side of the bricks, and the windows are dirty with cobwebs and dust, since it isn't a fully maintained building, and it's only ever occupied when a call comes in.

Over the years, I've heard countless stories from locals describing their experiences there, all relating to paranormal happenings and things that cannot be fully explained. I'm not aware of the firehouse's full history, and I can't give you any specific names or stories, but I know that a few members have lost their lives while on the job over the years, and many people believe that some of their spirits are still hanging around.

One woman I spoke to claimed to have seen an apparition. She'd been walking past the firehouse one evening when she felt as though she was being watched, and when she looked up, there was someone standing at the window, staring right at her. There were no active calls at the time, so there shouldn't have been anybody inside. But she was insistent that she had seen a man dressed in an old-fashioned fireman's garb watching her from the uppermost window. She described his stare as intense but not threatening, though the sight of him had definitely unnerved her. The woman had turned away and kept on walking, assuming she was merely imagining things. When she glanced back, the man was already gone, as though he had never been there at all.

Other stories I've heard range from seeing shadowy figures and hearing noises that can't be explained coming from within the firehouse. Since I live right next door, it's pretty easy for me to keep track of when there are people in the building or not, and a majority of the time, these experiences take place when the firehouse is empty, leaving no possible room for explanation.

I've had my own strange experiences too. On more than one occasion, while I've been out gardening in my front yard, I've heard voices spilling out through the firehouse's air conditioning vent, which faces my garden. One time I thought I heard someone crying out for help, but the firehouse was empty at the time, and there was nobody out on the street either. Sometimes I can hear a male voice speaking too, although it's always difficult to make out exactly what he's saying as the voice seems to fade and get louder without reason. I know for a fact that each time, the house has been empty, and there should be nobody inside speaking loud enough for me to hear them through the vent.

My nephew is a fireman himself, and he too has heard and seen things that he can't explain from the firehouse next door. He told me about the experience he'd had when he'd been inside the station alone one night. The others had all gone home, leaving him to check the equipment and lock up, since he lived right next door and it was his turn to do the usual rounds. He was certain he was alone as he'd watched everyone walk out the door. But as he was about to leave himself, he heard someone humming from deeper inside the firehouse. He thought it odd but assumed it might have been coming from outside rather than in the building itself. Nevertheless, he decided to check the station again to make sure nobody had come back without him realising. As he approached the locker room, where the sound seemed to be coming from, he saw a shadow disappear through the doorway, as though someone had quickly darted inside. But when he went to check, there was *nobody* there. He told me he'd been pretty spooked at that point, and got the feeling he wasn't alone, even though he was, as far as he could tell. He left as quickly as he could after that. I remember how shaken he seemed when he'd come home, and he told me the story that same night after I wheedled it out of him. I'd already known some of the rumours about the firehouse, so I had no qualms about believing him.

On another occasion, my son and I were out in the yard when we heard a door slam from inside the firehouse, even though the place was, as usual, completely empty. He ran to go and see who it was, thinking there might have been an emergency or one of the other guys had gone in, but there was nobody there, and the door was locked, meaning there couldn't have been anyone inside either. Neither of us could find an explanation for it, just like we couldn't really explain a lot of things we saw happen over there.

Some of the other firemen and women have claimed to see doors opening and closing on their own, have glimpsed shadowy figures that seem to disappear into thin air, and have heard footsteps in the building even when they're the only ones there. The number of different witnesses and accounts that have stemmed from the firehouse over the years only goes to show how haunted the place truly is. Given how dangerous the job is and how many lives have been lost over the years since it was built, I suppose it's no surprise that spirits still linger around the old building.

Even my son, a brave fireman, is now too afraid to go into the firehouse alone, especially on a night, after the strange things he has witnessed. So are most of the others he works with, who have also experienced unexplainable things while staying there after dark. They make it a point now to never lock up or leave someone there alone, especially when it's already gone dark.

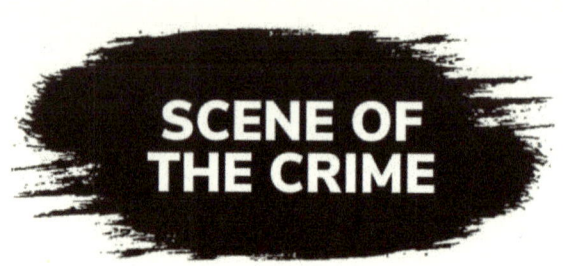

SCENE OF THE CRIME

The street sign glowed orange, almost making it seem as if it was lit from within rather than the streetlight reflecting off its surface. I knew this street well. It was not unlike many of the others around the city housing the poor, buildings in various states of disrepair, mostly a place best left forgotten by those who were lucky enough to escape from or avoided the pitfalls of life.

I didn't live here but my mind seemed to hold a permanent residence on it. It was here, six years before, that I remembered when I had discharged my firearm in the line of duty for the first time. A suspect in a drug trafficking investigation had been traced back to one of the buildings and we were there hoping to find him and make an arrest.

The whole thing went bad from the start. Later, it would come out that the man I saw sitting in the lobby had alerted the suspect by text message that we were in the building. Instead of the element of surprise being on our side and reducing the possibility of violence, the perp had a chance to arm himself which resulted in me having to fire my gun. It was a good shooting, everyone knew it, even me, but that didn't stop me from seeing the guy's face in my dreams for almost two years.

I hated going passed that building when I drew this patrol. If I could, I would skip it all together. The people that live on this block deserve better though than a guy pretending they don't exist in order to avoid bad memories so I pop up the lever signalling a right turn.

I can feel the tension in my hands and have to flex my fingers in an attempt to loosen the death grip I have on the steering wheel. The sweat that has accumulated on my hands makes it feel as if I am peeling each digit from the leather cover, but it does give me a temporary reprieve.

Off to my left I see it, the squat two story cement structure that represents one my worst days as an officer. It has been abandoned for three years now, put on some list for the city to demolish when they get around to it, meaning they have decided to "urbanize". Until then, it has become and will remain a cesspool for drug attics, squatters and animals that have found their way into its interior.

The best I can hope for is I don't see anyone staring out through the broken windows. If so, I can just drive by and pretend that I haven't been holding my breath for the last thirty seconds.

My eyes pass over the windows, the darkness behind them against the washed-out color of the concrete makes them look like huge eyes staring down at me. They taunt me, with their unflinching gaze.

One by one, I only see blank empty space. I've almost convinced myself that the building is either unbelievably empty or that the trespassers have the wherewithal to at least stay out of sight when a police cruiser is coming down the street. I hit the second to last windows when I see a face staring down at me.

I had basically moved on autopilot and passed by him as if he wasn't even there. But my brain screamed {Wait!}, and I found myself staring back at him for a moment before he retreated back into the interior of the building.

I was jostled back into the present when the front tire of my car bumped up against a curb as I sat there dumbly staring at the now empty window. Seeing someone wasn't something out of the ordinary, I'd gone inside a few times to run off a few people in my time. It was {who} I saw, or at least who I thought I'd seen that had the hairs on the back of my neck standing on end. That face had been permanently burned into my brain, it was the face of the man I'd shot, a man who had been dead for six years.

I considered ignoring what I'd clearly seen for a moment, after all, there was no way that it had been who I'd thought I'd seen. It was dark, and from the distance I was from the window it would be easy to make that kind of mistake.

{It could have just been a reflection, if not though it has to be someone else, maybe someone who looks just like them.} The thought made sense in my brain, but for some reason I just didn't buy the simplest explanation. In my gut, something told me it had been him, impossible as that was.

It took me a few attempts to park my car. First, I hit the curb again, the second time I overcorrected and was halfway out in the road before managing to maneuver the cruiser safely along the side of the road. My hands shook just reaching for the door handle. I'd heard plenty of stories, experiences from other officers of seeing and hearing things that couldn't be explained. I just took these as the result of too much stress and too little sleep. But now, confronted with something myself, I found myself afraid to step out of the car and walking into that building.

With great effort and a few deep breaths I forced my limbs to obey and got out of the car. Turning to look over at the structure, it seemed larger and more imposing than its two stories should be. The front door hung partially open, but was it an invitation or a trap? Both seemed equally likely.

I didn't want to find myself in a bad situation unprepared, so I unclipped my firearm and flicked on my flashlight even before reaching the opening. I pushed open the door the rest of the way and shined my flashlight into the dark space.

"Police officer!" I yelled as I swung the light back and forth. "Is someone here?"

The announcement was met by silence. There could have been a number of reasons for this, most of which weren't good, but it wasn't surprising. Not many people are going to come out with their hands up admitting they knew they weren't supposed to be there and were just leaving. I had reached the moment of truth, either I could leave or go find what I had seen in that window.

I knew what I had to do. I wanted to leave, but I had a job to do. If someone was here, it was up to me to do so.

With the first step through I was already regretting my decision, not just of coming inside, but my entire career choice. {Why in God's name would someone sign up to do this?}

As much as I hated to admit it to myself, I was hoping to be given some reason to bolt. In that first few feet, any odd noise and that would be out of there. Fortunately or unfortunately, that didn't happen which meant I made my way through the building to the stairway to the second floor.

As I made my way down the single hallway to the room in which I'd seen the face, I strained to hear any signs of another person being present. Other than the sounds I was making, the second floor remained quiet. I was sure that if someone else had been here, I would have heard them.

I finally reached the door to the room. I had to make a decision to either rush through the door, giving me the possible advantage of surprise or I could knock on the door and try a more subtle approach. I decided the latter option was the best choice given in all likelihood they already had heard me if someone was inside like I suspected.

I hit the door with three solid knocks. "This is the police."

As soon as I knocked on the door, I hear the sound of someone running. Drawing my sidearm, I reach out and try the handle, expecting it to be locked but find it turns easily in my hand. I turn quickly into the room, my light and gun swinging to every corner of the room seeking out the source of the footsteps that have mysteriously gone quiet.

After a few seconds for my eyes to adjust, the lights outside give me enough ambient light to see by. I can see that the room is empty, and the window is shut but a door is located on the wall to the right. My sidearm at the ready I move towards it, ready to defend myself if necessary.

Standing off to the side I reach out and knock on the door. "This is the police. Whoever is in there, I need you to come out now with your hands on your head."

My order is met with silence. Reaching out I grab the handle and swing the door open expecting something to happen but there is no sign of compliance or violence of any kind. Instead, there is nothing. I peer around the corner of the frame and see an empty supply closet.

I quickly spin around, searching the room once more. The room is still empty and as far as I can tell I'm alone. That's when what I can only describe a cold finger brush against my back of my neck. I turn, gun at the ready, but no one is there. I back away from the empty closet, unwilling to take my eyes from it. As soon as I pass through the doorframe I turn and run. I don't stop until I reach my patrol car and have locked myself safely inside.

As I pull away from the building, I risk a glance up at the window. I don't see anyone there, but I can feel his eyes on me, watching.

FINDING THE SCENT

The beams of multiple flashlights cut back and forth disappearing briefly as they passed behind the dense growth of trees we were searching. Ruby, my bloodhound and search and rescue dog, strained against her leash with her nose press against the decaying vegetation of the forest floor. I had long since learned to trust her when she was following the invisible path only traceable by her ultra-sensitive nose.

We were looking for the remains of a young man who had been last seen in this area almost a week ago. The parents still held out hope, that we would find their son alive. It was still possible, but with every passing day it was becoming increasingly likely the best we could do was give them closure and a chance to mourn their child.

The flashlight in my hand bounced with every step I took as Ruby pulled me deeper into the woods. She was being pulled away from the search group and was starting to get the feeling I was going to have to reign her in.

I let her go a few hundred more feet before I finally gave the lead a tug expecting her to heed my wordless command. Instead, it doubled her determination to get to wherever she was going. With a mighty lunge, the end of the leash was ripped from my hand and Ruby took off into the darkness.

I stood there staring off in the direction she had

run, confused, and stunned. This type of behavior was totally out of character. Ruby was the dog that didn't chase other animals and obeyed commands almost instantly. For her to ignore me the way she did, that made no sense. Even as a green K9 Officer, she had never been disobedient.

Not only was she my partner, Ruby had become a member of my family. I had to find her.

"Ruby! Here girl! Ruby!"

I cupped my ear trying to listen for the sound of her charging towards my voice. I could hear the leaves rustling in the wind and a few birds above me but no dog.

"Damn Rube, what got into you?" I whispered into the dead evening.

I had to let my C.O. know what had happened even though I knew what his reaction was going to be. He would berate me for not keeping control of my animal. After a few stern remarks I was told to "Go find the dog.". I told him I was on it and began moving my way in the direction I'd last seen her going.

With every passing minute I began to get more and more worried. The distance she could travel made my area of search larger and larger. It was bad enough we'd been out here to find a missing person, now I had a missing K9 too.

A stick breaking to my left draws my attention and I see Ruby standing there. She's staring at something, but from my angle I can't tell or see what it is. I receive a brief looks in my direction before turning her attention back to whatever has sparked her interest.

I start to move slowly towards her hoping not to trigger whatever had caused her to run in the first place. If I can only make it to the leash, I'll be able to at least bring her back to the car before I resume the search without her.

Two minutes have passed before I cover the fifty feet that lie between us. I'm pretty sure I can jump and grab the leash at this point, but I hesitate. Now that I'm right next to Ruby, I can hear her. A mix between a whine and a growl is coming from her as she stares directly ahead of her. I'm not even sure she knows I am there.

I'm curious what she sees so I move my way over next to her. All I can do is stare right along with her. In front of me is a small hole that at some point had been covered in wood. The planks look like there in bad shape from exposure to the weather and time. There's a hole in the center of the cover where something has broken through. It isn't the hole that has our attention though, but what is floating above it.

The best I can tell it is some sort of cloud or mist that doesn't have any form that I can make out. It's just sitting there, and the oddest thing of all, it is glowing.

I rub my eyes, sure that I must be seeing things, I have to be. What's in front of me can't be real. These things don't exist in the real world.

The "cloud" floats there, unmoving for a few more seconds before it loses some of its luster and begins to descend into the hole and out of sight. When it passes out of sight I run forward at a dead sprint, stopping only when I reach the edge of the wooden planks.

I don't want to test my weight on the rotten wood so I lean over as far as I can and try and shine my light down inside the hole. The wooden square is large enough that I can't make out the entire interior but from what I can see mist seems to be gone. I have a bad feeling of what the hole might mean. The battle raging in my head between the desire to look down and bodily harm is a close call, but curiosity wins out in the end.

I get down on my hands and knees and scooch myself towards the opening. The planks groan in protest, but they somehow hold my weight. I hold the light out over the opening and look down. It takes only a second for my eyes to register that the mist has disappeared, but it's what is at the bottom that has my breath frozen in my lungs. It's a body.

A few hours later the body of the young man we had been searching for had been recovered from down below. It was a tragic end to a search, even if it was an expected one. Something had drawn Ruby towards that spot in the forest, one we had no plan to be in. I think that mist must have been the spirit of the young man, calling out in the only way he could, crying out to be found.

INVISIBLE PERPETRATOR

I became a detective because I crave answers. I've always had a talent for weaving together clues, taking a fragmented image, and putting the pieces together. It gives me immense satisfaction to crack a case and see the guilty parties meet justice. I'm good at my job and I love it. But there's one story that haunts me, one question I could never answer, no conclusion that logic could ever lead me to…

This happened in the early 1980s when I was still a beat cop with the Oklahoma City Police Department. One week I noticed that several officers' cars had Ghostbusters stickers stuck to the windows. I was confused and asked one of the guys what was with all the Ghostbuster stuff. It seemed unprofessional in my opinion, but who was some rookie to pass judgment. His explanation to my question, however, was even stranger than the details themselves.

He told me that a few officers had been on a call recently where the occupants had complained of paranormal activity. When they called 911, the dispatcher initially told them not to waste her time, but the caller was so adamant and seemed so genuinely afraid, she finally sent a cruiser over to check it out.

My buddy was skeptical, even made jokes at the family's expense as he and his partner made their way over. I couldn't blame him, it sounded like a ridiculous waste of valuable time and resources to me. They expected to see a family of drug addicts tweaking out when they got there and took their time driving over.

He said that when the officers arrived at the house, the residents were outside, terrified, while the sounds of banging doors and shattering glass came from inside the house. The officers were shocked. They were still unconvinced that something paranormal was occurring, of course, but were surprised that it was anything more than drug-addled paranoia. However, it seemed like there really was a break-in of some sort, so they called for backup as the family cowered near the car.

Still assuming it was an intruder inside, they brought a canine, Red, to help clear the property. Now, Red was the meanest damn dog you ever saw. He got his name for the number of times he drew blood, let's put it that way. Yet, when they brought him up toward the front door, he absolutely refused to go inside the home. He growled and whined but would not set a paw inside. With his ears low and his tail tucked between his legs, Red stubbornly grounded himself, refusing to be moved. It was unprecedented.

Finally realizing that the dog would be of no use, two officers approached each of the homes' doors, front and back, with their guns drawn. One waited outside, keeping his eyes out in case the intruder tried to make a break for it. That one officer was the friend from whom I heard the story.

The crashing and banging noises had continued throughout the entire ordeal, reaching a fever pitch. It sounded like there was a tornado inside, he said. However, as soon as the officers busted through the doors into the house, the noises came to a sudden halt. As an eerie silence fell, my buddy prepared to make chase, expecting the criminal to come tearing out of the house at any second. Instead, nothing but more silence.

The officers had been inside for a while, too long, and my friend became worried. He decided to follow them inside. When he stepped through the door he was stunned. Everything inside was destroyed. Furniture smashed to splinters, food from the fridge tossed around like confetti, framed pictures smashed, and even holes punched through the drywall. It was absolute chaos but there was no one around.

The officers had been searching every room, corner, and cabinet in the house. One even crawled beneath the house to check the crawl space. Nothing. My friend had been standing outside as the others entered and would have seen if someone ran out of the house. It was a crime without a criminal. They were at a loss.

The residents claimed the sounds had suddenly started up when they were inside and had no idea what caused them. They said they had been experiencing escalating events, strange noises that turned to misplaced objects that turned to dark shadows in the night.

That story always gave me the creeps. None of the other guys ever really talked about what happened because they were afraid everyone would think they were crazy. I can understand why. It's impossible, yet by all accounts, it's true. The family ended up selling the house. The next person who bought it had it demolished. Now it's a convenience store. Every time I pass by the lot, however, I feel a twinge of discomfort and agitation. I like answers and conclusions. I want the story wrapped up with a bow and a perp sitting in jail, to boot. I don't believe in ghosts.

All that said, the story for lack of a better word, haunts me. I suppose, just this once, I need to be okay with not knowing the truth. Or maybe, I do, and I'm just too stubborn to admit it.

IMPRISONMENT

My father was in prison for most of my life. He was an addict and a dealer in his youth and ended up getting himself in a lot of trouble. After his first conviction, he got out of prison and had me. He tried to go on the straight and narrow but it was difficult. He relapsed and ended up getting locked up again. From then on he was in and out of prison until his death.

My mom was a superhero. She took great care of me and eventually remarried. I still wanted a relationship with my father, however, so from time to time we would write letters to one another. He told me often how he wanted a better life for me than he had, warning me that prison was worse than imaginable.

"When your body's in a cage," he said, "your mind is too. I swear sometimes I'm losing it." That was the last line in the last letter he ever sent me. He was found dead in his cell the next day, causes undetermined.

I promised myself I would do better for my future children than my dad was able to do for me. I joined the army and swore that I would build a life to be proud of. Most of all, I vowed that I would never, ever step foot in a prison. Fate has a funny sense of humor though.

As part of my Reserve training, I had to pull a twelve-hour shift in Corrections. It was a strange feeling, walking through the doors of the prison. I wondered if my dad had ever been there, locked up in a cell.

Our county facility is old; shockingly so. I felt uneasy as I walked across the dusty concrete floors. Anyway, it was a med-call, so the nurse had opened the little clinic, and we went to each cellblock and had inmates line up to get their medication. It was easy enough and no one gave us any trouble. I was starting to relax, finally.

After that was finished, the nurse left, the clinic was closed, and all of the inmates were back in their blocks. I secured the last block, and as I turned back towards the clinic, I saw something that made my heart leap into my throat. It was a shadow on the floor, someone quickly crossing back to the clinic. Remembering my training, I remained as calm as I could. I dashed around the corner, thinking an inmate had managed to avoid being secured and was sneaking into the clinic. I couldn't believe I'd made such a stupid mistake. However, when I turned the corner, there was no one there. The shadow had been absolutely distinct and there was no doubt in my mind about what I'd seen. I walked the block, accounting a second time for all of the inmates. None were missing. Now, my head was spinning.

I went back upstairs and explained to the officers what happened, trying to play it cool, but deep down I was rattled. One of the other COs laughed and said, "Oh, that's just Mrs. Gray. She's been hanging around here for years!"

I just stared back, confused. Was he serious? Apparently, he was. There was a long history of strange shadows slinking around corners. Silhouetted figures that disappeared when approached. Nothing to worry about, they promised me. I could hardly believe what they were telling me.

When I returned home that night my head hurt. It was swimming with stories of prisons and ghosts. More than anything, I thought of my father. I wasn't sure what I had seen up there at the corrections facility. Whether it was Mrs. Gray or a figment of my imagination was up for debate, but in those short few hours at the prison, I felt like I had lost my mind. As I fell into a fitful sleep that night my father's last words rang in my ears. "When your body's in a cage, your mind is too."

I finally understood what he meant, and for a moment in that prison, I thought I was losing my sanity too.

HOLY FIRE

I'm a firefighter in Cleveland, Ohio. It's sort of a family profession. Both my father and his brother were firefighters too, and even their father was a volunteer way back in the day. As a child, there was never a question in my mind about what I wanted to do when I grew up. Then, I did, and I made it happen. Now, as a grown man with sons of my own, I can truly say that I love my job and I'm proud of the work I do. It is dangerous though, and as a father and a husband, I often worry about what my family would do if something happened to me.

I shared these concerns with my mother. My dad has since passed, unrelated to the job. I asked her if she ever worried about my dad when he was at work. She was quiet for a long time before answering, and when she finally spoke, I was surprised by what she said.

"No," she told me, "because I always prayed that he would be safe. And God listened to me. I pray for you too, son, and the Lord listens. I don't think anything bad is going to happen to you." Now, I'm not as religious as my mother, but there was something comforting about her confidence. It put me at ease.

The very next day I was responding to a call in a dark, secluded, industrial area at night. The streets were empty and we were screaming down the road in the truck when the engine suddenly sputtered, stalled, and coasted to a stop. Nothing like this had ever happened before, and we exchanged confused glances. That's when I noticed we were right in front of a railroad crossing with no gates, less than two feet from the tracks. Just as we stopped, quite literally seconds later, a freight train came barrelling through. Stunned, we watched the train speed past the very spot we would have been, had the truck not inexplicably stopped. There were no gates to lower, no lights to warn, not even a whistle. We could feel the force of the train as it rushed past us, shaking the giant fire truck with its speed. I couldn't believe our luck. There is no question in my mind that I would have died that night if things had gone a little bit differently.

To all of our surprise, the engine sputtered back as soon as the train passed. The whole thing happened in a matter of minutes and, for the first time in my career, I really felt like I saw my life flash before my eyes. As we shook off our shock and continued on to complete the call, I said a prayer. Just in case.

The next morning my mother called me. She asked if everything was okay and seemed worried. I told her about the experience at the train tracks the night before and heard her gasp slightly. She told me that after going to bed early, she woke in the middle of the night in a panic. She wasn't sure why, but she felt compelled to pray, specifically for me. So she did. When she was finished with her prayer she felt once again at ease and went back to sleep. The strangest part is that when I asked her what time she awoke, she told me it was close to midnight. I gulped. That had been the same exact time the train had passed us by. After that, I made it a point to pray before I left for work every day. I really do believe my mother's faith saved me that night, and it wasn't the last time.

A few years later I received a call to a highway construction site for a burning shanty. It was a blazing Sunday afternoon, during a summer heatwave, and fires had been springing up all over town. We pulled up and began advancing the handline when it suddenly seemed like the hose became tangled up in the hose bed. We couldn't extend it far enough to get close to the burning structure. Frustrated, I ran around to check the line. Everything seemed to be as it should and I instructed my buddy to pull harder. He did and still the hose sat firmly in place. I was dumbfounded. It didn't make any sense.

Just then I heard a whoosh of air, then the sound of an explosion. Even from afar, I could feel the heat of the blast hit me like a ton of fiery bricks. I looked around the corner of the truck to confirm what I already knew. The shanty had combusted in a fiery blast, sending pieces of white-hot wooden shrapnel flying into the air, and turning the structure into a smouldering pile of ash in seconds. Had me or one of my men been any closer, we would have been caught in the explosion, meaning sure death. Of course, seconds after the explosion, the hose was released. It hurts me to this day to think about what would have happened had the handline not malfunctioned, or the truck not stalled out in front of the tracks. When I called my mother that night to tell her what happened at the shanty, she already knew. The same urge to pray had come over her. It was unexplainable, but it was the truth. Whether it was my mom, or God, or the Universe, some force spared my life that day for the second time.

I retired at the end of that year. I had a great run with the department, followed in my father's footsteps, even saved lives; but it was my time. I had kids that I wanted to see grow up and a wife who didn't deserve to be a widow. I wasn't ready to test my luck a third time. I look back on my time as a firefight with fondness and gratitude. Despite no longer putting myself in daily danger, however, one thing hasn't changed since I left my job. I pray every single day.

VINCE FRANK BELL

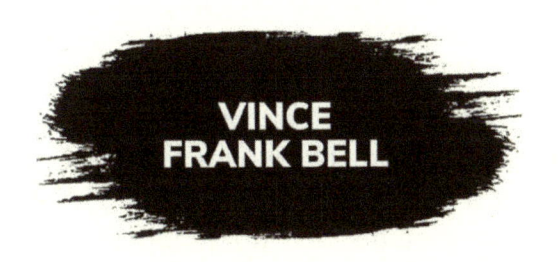

I responded to a call to a man-down, breathing status unknown. We pulled up to a bar. It was the divey type with neon beer brand signs and a dusty old pool table. It wasn't my first time being called to that location, as it's known for fights and assaults. When we arrived, there were no police on the scene. Everything was still and empty and it was just past midnight. A man was standing outside smoking a cigarette. He looked calm, too calm. His eyes were kind of glazed over like he was far away. Without a hint of emotion, he spoke. "There's a guy on the floor in there."

I walked inside and found a man, or rather, the corpse of a man. It was a gruesome scene. The body was splayed out on top of that dirty pool table, limbs at unnatural angles. Blood covered the green felt and splattered the white cue ball. The man was beyond bloody, his white T-shirt drenched with sticky red liquid. His eyes were open, frozen in the last expression he ever made, full of fear. The whites of his eyes had become a lurid pale purple in color. He had dried blood on his face, dripping into his open mouth. The cause of death was immediately evident, multiple stab wounds. Over twenty at least and most of them in the chest, directly in his heart. He obviously wasn't breathing. Clearly, he had been dead for a while. We pronounced him there on the scene, and I found his drivers' license with his name on it. His name was unique, so it stuck with me. Vince Frank Bell. I never learned exactly what happened at the bar that night. I would imagine a drunken brawl got out of hand. A waste of precious life if you ask me, for a man to die like that in a dirty old dive bar. Of all my experiences as an EMT it was the one, still is the one, that remains with me. The story doesn't end there, though…

Two weeks later, I was sitting in the back of my ambulance, taking inventory of our IV supplies. Suddenly, the lights went off in the back. This had never happened before and though it wasn't inherently frightening, I felt the hairs on the back of my neck stand up. I can't explain why but for some reason I felt like I was no longer alone. Then, to my horror, I heard a small whisper. It was faint, almost imperceptible, and completely unexplainable.

Now, the fact of the matter is I've always believed in ghosts. I know it's strange to say, especially as someone who is often surrounded by the dead and dying, but it's the truth. So, I responded accordingly, to the best of my ability I pulled out my phone and turned on my voice recorder. With a gulp, I asked…" Who's here with me?"

I let my voice recorder run and sat very still, eyes closed, listening. For what was about two minutes, but felt like a lifetime, I waited in silence. The tiny metal-enclosed space seemed to vibrate with energy, or maybe I was just shaking. In there, with my eyes closed, I could feel the presence of someone there with me. I didn't dare open my eyes, afraid of what I might see. Instead, I just listened, waiting patiently. Nothing but silence greeted me.

Finally, the lights in the ambulance snapped back on. With a sigh of relief, I opened my eyes, the strange sensation, the fear and panic, all melting away. This job was getting to me, I thought. I needed to take some time off. At the end of my shift, I requested the weekend to myself, not telling my supervisor exactly why. He could tell something was off, so he agreed, and I went home that night ready to relax and forget the whole thing.

As I was lying in bed, scrolling through social media before I hit the lights and tried to get some sleep, I suddenly remembered the recording I made. Though I heard nothing in that ambulance, I felt compelled to listen back, for whatever reason. So, I opened the file and hit play. Then, I leaned back, closed my eyes, and listened.

There was no sound except the crackle of the mic and my rapid breathing. Of course not, I thought. I had just been paranoid after all. As the recording counted down to the end, I opened my eyes and prepared to click it off. That's when I heard something that made my blood run cold.

In the very last seconds of the audio, I could hear a whisper. Faint, like the first one I heard, only much clearer. As if someone had been speaking directly into the microphone. It was the deep baritone of a man, his voice crackling with a smoker's gravel. I was so shocked and afraid I almost threw my phone across the room. But it wasn't the voice itself that was so frightening. It was what it said. There was no explanation, no logic to what I was hearing, yet as I played it back, I only became more confident in what I heard. The whispering man said a name. A unique name; first, middle, and last. A name I will never forget as long as I live. Vince Frank Bell.

NIGHT AT THE CASINO

I was working as an EMT and security officer at a casino. I was the newbie. There was always a bit of playful hazing among the staff when somebody joined the team, and as someone who perhaps takes myself a little too seriously at times, it wasn't my favorite part of the job. The other security officers would often send me to deal with the drunkest and most belligerent customers, or tell scary stories about ghosts that roamed the halls when no one else was around. I tried to brush it off and do my job. I was there for a paycheck, after all, not to make friends.

One day, about two weeks into the gig, I was walking the parking structure around 0300 hours. Up the hill, by the top-level of the garage, were some street lights, a guard rail, and a road leading up to a water tower, but nothing else. As I made my rounds, I noticed that night seemed especially dark somehow, the street lights dimmer than usual. Still, through the dark, I caught sight of a figure.

It was tough to make out, appearing to be dressed in all black, almost like a walking shadow. I felt a shiver travel down my spine. Usually, nothing scares me. I'm a big guy and almost always armed with a weapon of some kind. If anything, I should be the one people are afraid to encounter on a dark evening. Still, something about the figure just felt... off. I couldn't tell if it was looking down the hill at me or up the hill towards the tower, their face obscured. In either case, the figure was still as stone, just staring off in one direction.

"Hey!" I called out, trying my best to sound threatening. I was shocked to hear that my voice was shaking. What had come over me, I wondered. The figure didn't respond. No turn, no movement, no reply. Only stillness and silence. My heart began to beat faster I didn't have a flashlight on me so I decided to go grab one before investigating. Keeping my eyes on the figure the entire time, I went down one level and met up with another officer and told him about what I'd seen, secretly hoping he'd come with me to confront them "Aw, you need a nightlight, big boy?" he teased.

I seethed but took the flashlight anyway, determined to figure out what the hell was going on. It'd been some time now and the silhouette was still immobile, my gaze trained on the hill where they stood. The other officer made another snarky comment as I started off with the flashlight and with a flash of anger I turned around to snap back.

"Fuck off and do your job," I told him. He got quiet after that. When I turned back around, however, the figure was gone. Not only that, but the dim lights seemed to have returned to normal, the moon once again illuminating the previously pitch-black hill. I turned around, wanting to ask the other officer if he had seen it too. His expression answered for me. Our momentary squabble forgotten, we stared at each other in matching shock.

That officer and I did end up becoming friends eventually, against all odds. Perhaps that night had something to do with it. I found out later that there had been a number of sightings in the area and on levels 5-7 of the garage. It wasn't all hazing, there really was something strange happening at that place. Both of us had a handful of other unexplainable encounters throughout our time there, until the building eventually burned down in a massive fire. Apparently, when the casino was put in they had to move an old Indian cemetery and the sightings started soon after that. It was believed by many in the nearby town that it had been cursed because of that. Believe what you will about the casino and the burial ground but I know one thing for certain. That was no prank I witnessed, but something much darker. Something that made me afraid.

WEEPING JESUS

I've seen a lot of strange things during my ten years as a firefighter. Even in a small town like mine, this job brings you face to face with some of the stranger aspects of life. A forest fire that began with a little kid trying to kill ants with a magnifying glass, refracting the light until the dry brush ignited. A blaze set to cover up the scene of a gruesome crime. I've even gotten a couple of calls for the cliche cat stuck in a tree situation. The strangest thing by far, however, happened when I was still just a rookie.

About seven or eight years ago, we arrived at a townhouse with heavy fire from the first floor on side one. Someone had fallen asleep with a frozen pizza in the toaster oven. Luckily, the residents managed to make it out before it was too late, and as they received oxygen from the EMT's we set about putting out the flames.

After making entry, locating the fire in the kitchen, and extinguishing it, we set about taking out a few windows for ventilation. After the smoke had risen, we noticed that the living area to the rear of the kitchen (which was on the right-hand side as we entered) had taken significant smoke and heat damage. All of the furniture was badly singed, if not completely reduced to ash. The walls were streaked black with smoke. The only thing that looked unharmed by the fire was a framed image, hanging above the mantle.

On the wall was a picture of Jesus Christ, the only object in the room that appeared untouched. It defied the laws of smoke and fire, and the strangest thing of all is that even the wall BEHIND the picture was smoke-stained and blistered. For lack of a better word, it seemed miraculous. But that wasn't all…

There was evidence of two streams of water that had trickled from the painting to a point in the middle of the wall where they met and continued down to the floor. Upon closer examination, it looked almost as if the image of Christ was weeping, the bubbled marks of water the only damage on the canvas, streaming forth from the eyes of the Holy man. My friend, another rookie firefighter, was the first to notice. He muttered something in Spanish and crossed himself, sending up a prayer of thanks. Being more logical than spiritual, I sought an explanation. Perhaps spray from the hose or even steam.

The odd thing was that the line had been pulled through this room and was flowing into the kitchen to push the fire out the front, through a large, vented window. No water had been moving through the room, and the steam produced had been pushed out the window. Still, I was skeptical. I was curious to hear what the Fire Marshall would say. However, to my surprise, even he was amazed.

"The greatest anomaly of my career," is what he called it.

The woman who owned the townhouse was a devout Christian. When we told her about the painting she fell to her knees, weeping. She said Christ saved her life. It was difficult to argue with.

Later, the local paper wrote about the fire. When they interviewed the homeowner, she told them about the painting, and how she believed her faith saved her that day. The journalist confirmed with the Fire Marshall and the story became a piece of local lore. Everyone in our sleepy little town knew about weeping Jesus, as he came to be known. The Catholic church nearby even claimed it as a miracle, and worshipers from neighboring cities would travel to see the burned-up townhouse.

The woman who owned the house, and the painting, kept it above her bed until her dying day. She passed away recently of old age. Her memorial was attended by many community members, and I felt compelled to pay my respects. I learned not too long after that the woman had a plan for the painting after her passing. She gave it to the local fire department.

Now, the unblemished image of weeping Jesus hangs in a prominent place in our little firehouse, serving as both a lucky charm and a reminder that miracles are possible. While I am not a woman of faith, I can't help but look up at the image's softly smiling face and wonder… Did Christ really save a life that day?

RUN AWAY

When I was a municipal cop, I was sent to a missing person runaway juvenile call. The town I worked in was inner city and poor, and it wasn't uncommon for children to go missing or run off, unfortunately. Even more horribly, it wasn't unheard of that parents would make their children… disappear, in some way or another. It was a tough place to work and because of that, I was rarely fazed. Except for this one night.

This call was a little different than usual because it was one of the better streets in town, and the family was squared away. The husband and wife were both educators and known in their church and community to be loving and generous. They had two daughters, the older of which was the one who had gone missing. When I arrived the family was in shambles, understandably. The mother had woken up in the middle of the night and decided to check on the girls. When she opened the door to the older daughter's room she was greeted by an open window and an empty bed.

I asked the parents if they thought their daughter might have run away. It didn't seem likely to me, given the circumstances, so I was surprised when the couple exchanged a shifty glance. I narrowed my eyes and pushed a little harder. What was it? Did she have a boyfriend they didn't approve of? Was she showing signs of mental stress? Had she ever talked about going somewhere else? To every question, the partners answered no, but I could tell they were holding something back.

"Did she seem unhappy or discontented in any way?" I asked, getting frustrated. They again exchanged a strange look. I reminded them gruffly that I couldn't help them unless they helped me. The mother began to sob.

"You're going to think we're crazy," she said. I felt my stomach twist. Before I could figure out what she meant by that, however, the younger tottered into the room, a teddy bear still clasped in her little hand.

"Daddy," she said, "I see grandma in the hall."

With that, she pointed down the long, unlit hallways off the living room where we were seated. I looked in the direction she was gesturing but saw nothing. When I looked back at the parents they were as white as sheets. The father leapt to his feet and raced down the hall, turning on every light he could find as he did so. His behavior was strange, and I started to feel more and more uneasy.

When he returned a few moments later he looked ill. He took his seat and looked up at me with wild eyes. "Officer, did you see her? Did you see my mother?"

I told him I had not, and asked him why it was remarkable that his mother had walked down the hallway. The husband pressed his palms against his face and shook his head before he replied. "She died last year," he finally admitted. "And I know how this sounds, I really do, but…we see her walking around the house all the time." I gulped. That was a first.

"If our daughter ran away, that's why," the wife said through her tears. "She saw his mother, the thing, first. It terrifies her. She says she can't sleep at night. She says she doesn't want to live in a haunted house."

Their story was strange, to say the least. At the time I was unconvinced by anything they said. I requested they come down to the station to answer a couple more questions. They hesitantly agreed, and as I led the couple and their second child down the driveway to my cruiser, I turned and looked back at the house one last time. What I saw made me feel sick.

For just a fleeting moment, I swear I saw an old woman standing in the upstairs window, her bony frame backlit by the lights that the father left on. Then, I blinked, and she was gone. I tried to brush it off, remain professional, and keep my cool. Someone noticed, however. It was the little girl. She looked up at me with big blue eyes and asked, "Did you see grandma too?"

It still gives me goosebumps to think about that house and that night. It turns out that the teenage daughter had snuck out because she couldn't sleep. She'd been doing it for weeks, just taking walks around the park before coming home at daylight. Her parents were relieved beyond measure, and I warned her not to do something so dangerous ever again. She agreed, and as she walked away from the station with her family, back to that terrifying place, I couldn't blame the girl for wanting to run away. I too had seen the face of the old woman in the window. I didn't sleep for a week.

LONG FORGOTTEN

My uncle works as a dispatcher in my town, and he recently told my family and I about one of the weirdest calls he's ever gotten in the whole of his career. I have to admit, after he told me about it, I couldn't stop thinking about it for days afterwards, and it still freaks me out when I remember it.

It was fairly late at night, maybe between 11pm to midnight, when he received a call from a local landline number. When he answered it, however, there was only static on the other end, as though the connection hadn't fully gone through. After unsuccessfully trying to reach out to the person on the other side of the line, the call cut off and he assumed it had merely been a mistake or a prank. Over the next hour, however, the same thing happened another two times. There wasn't anything wrong on his end, since he'd received calls in between that had gone through perfectly fine. But the same landline called three times, and every time he answered, he was met with nothing but crackling static. There wasn't even the semblance of a voice on the other side, just plain white noise. Once things had quietened down, he eventually called a squad to go and check the address, which he'd managed to trace from the caller ID. The fact that they had attempted to call three times suggested that there might actually be an emergency, but for some reason the caller had been unable to get through.

It was only afterwards that he heard about what came of the call from the landline, and the squad that he sent there. And it's a story that has bothered him ever since.

According to one of the officers who were dispatched to investigate the call, the house was seemingly unoccupied when they first got there. None of the lights were switched on, the curtains were drawn, and all of the doors and windows were locked. Nobody answered from inside, no matter how many times they knocked and announced their presence. Thinking something might have happened to incapacitate the caller, they made the decision to break the door open and force their way into the building.

Once they were in, the first thing they noticed was the smell. The heavy, rotting stench of something that had died long ago.

From their initial observation, the place had been untouched for a while. A thick layer of dust caked every surface, and one of the officers was sure he'd heard rats scuttling in the walls as they'd searched the house. The place stunk of damp and mildew, but it was nothing compared to the horrible smell of a decaying corpse. They would have thought the house completely vacant if not for that smell.

They found the body in the living room, sitting in an old leather armchair that was also caked in dust and grime.

Covering his nose to ward off the stench, the officer had used his flashlight to inspect the body. Although it was heavily decomposed, he was able to determine that it was a man somewhere in his mid to late eighties. He seemed to have died from natural causes judging from their preliminary examination, as there was no sign of any external injuries or wounds. The coroner was later able to clarify that he'd died of a heart attack while sitting in his chair, and no foul play had been involved.

They immediately requested an ambulance to take the body away, although it was clear he'd been dead for a while. They found out afterwards that the man had actually been dead for over five months, steadily wasting away in the darkness of his own home. Nobody had checked up on him or called the police during that time to express concern about him, and after a brief investigation, it was found that he had no family left alive. He'd died alone and forgotten about.

That isn't the strangest or most disturbing part of the story, however, because the question still remained: who had called dispatch? Someone must have placed the call, and the landline phone responsible had been traced to the inside of the house. Yet when the police did a full sweep of the house, they found nobody else there. There wasn't a single footprint or mark in the dust to suggest anybody had been in the house recently either. And there was no way anyone could have left after placing the call, since all the doors and windows were locked from the inside. The only other person who could have called for help was the dead man. Which, of course, was impossible.

What bothered the officer even more was the fact that the house had no running electricity. It turned out that all of the utilities in the house had been shut off when the resident had stopped paying the bills, after his death. Nothing worked, and nor had it worked for a long time. The landline had no way of operating, and yet somehow it had been used to place a call to the police.

The phone itself had been found in the hallway, still plugged in. But when the officer picked up the receiver, there wasn't a dial tone on the other end, and nothing happened when he tried punching a number into the dial pad. The phone was completely dead. Nor had it been disturbed recently. When they dusted for fingerprints, there was nothing to be found.

It was almost as though a call had never been placed, but the record existed in the dispatcher's files, and it had brought those officers to that very house where the dead man was.

It remains a mystery to this day who had placed the call and how they had managed it without a working phone. But in the end, who knows how long that dead body would have stayed there if they hadn't. Maybe that's all that really matters.

DUMMY

My mom was a 911 dispatcher back in the 90s. I was around seven years old at the time, but when I got older and more curious, I started asking her about some of the calls that she could still recall from that time. She told me about one in particular that was really bad, and still makes her feel terribly uneasy when she thinks about it.

She was working one year on the night of Halloween. She told me that Halloween tended to be one of the busiest nights for police and ambulance services, since many people took it as an opportunity to be more reckless and dangerous than any other night of the year. She'd taken a lot of calls already that night, but this one stuck out the most.

It was around 10 or 11pm when a call came in from a young woman. When my mom asked what the emergency was, she explained that there were a couple of guys driving around town with some kind of dummy or mannequin dragging behind their truck. The dummy itself was falling apart as it was dragged over the tarmac, and pieces of clothing and chunks of plastic were being torn off and scattered all over the roads of the city. It wasn't doing any harm as it was, but there was a risk that the dummy could fall off and cause an accident, plus the woman said that the sight was rather gruesome in the dark and might cause some disturbances if others saw it.

Given that it was Halloween, the most likely explanation was that the whole thing was a prank, since it was exactly the kind of thing that kids would use to scare people for a joke. My mom made a note of the incident, but there were more urgent calls to attend to first, so she didn't act on it right away. As the night went on, however, more and more calls started coming in about the truck dragging along this disintegrating dummy all around the city. It seemed to be upsetting people quite a bit, so she eventually sent out a patrol car to try and find the truck and put an end to the charade.

As they were driving around, looking for the truck, the police officers came across several articles of clothing and bits of plastic that had fallen off, but no sign of the dummy itself. When they eventually managed to catch up to the truck down and flag it down, they made a horrifying discovery.

The dummy turned out to not be a dummy at all. It was a person. A dead body, to be exact.

The guys driving the truck claimed to be completely ignorant of the body stuck to the back of their truck, and after some questioning and retracing their activities of the night, the truth was finally revealed, and it was worse than anyone could have realised.

The two guys had gone to a store earlier that evening to pick up some alcohol and snacks for the rest of the night. As they left, they had unknowingly backed the truck into an elderly man who had been standing behind them in their blind spot. Somehow, the man's clothing had gotten caught on the truck's rear bumper, and when they'd drove off, they'd taken the man with them.

These two men never even knew that they had been driving around in their truck, dragging this old man's body around town for miles, while people who saw it merely thought they were towing along a plastic dummy.

I can't even imagine what kind of pain that poor man had gone through in the moments before he died, unable to claw himself free from the back of the truck as he was dragged over the tarmac at horrifying speeds. Those pieces of clothing and plastic that people thought had belonged to a dummy were actually the clothing, flesh and body parts of that old man, being scattered around the whole city. When they finally got him free, his body had been in a gruesome state, completely and irrevocably broken. It must have been a horrible job for the officers who had to go back and find all of the pieces of him on the streets and the road.

Just thinking about it still gives me chills, and my mom told me it was one of the worst calls she'd ever taken when she found out what had happened afterwards. Nothing like that had ever happened to her since.

But the story doesn't end there. What's even weirder is that, when the paramedics arrived to attend to what was left of the man's body, one of them claimed to see an elderly man standing by the truck, just watching them. It was dark and they were unable to see who it was, but the figure turned and walked off into the field by the side of the road and seemed to just disappear into thin air. Nobody knew who the man was, but it almost seemed as though he had been waiting there until the paramedics came, and then he'd simply… vanished.

Given the amount of damage his body sustained throughout the whole ordeal, the man was proclaimed DOA (dead on arrival) at the hospital, and the two guys riding the truck were arrested and convicted of involuntary manslaughter.

INSIDE

I was on my way home after visiting my mother. It was the middle of March and an unseasonably warm night, so the walk was more enjoyable than normal. It was around a quarter to eleven at night, and the streets were pretty empty. It was quiet too, other than the warm breeze blowing down the road. I had only planned to stop by at home long enough to check my mail and change my clothes before heading back out, since I had other plans that night too.

I turned onto Saxton, heading for my building near Jordan. In the distance, I could see some red and blue flashing lights, and as I drew closer towards them, I noticed two police cruisers were parked out in front of my apartment. My place had already been broken into on two separate occasions in the past. The apartment was on the cheaper side of the market, so security wasn't as high-tech as a lot of places, making it a common target for thieves and burglars in the area. I'd already upgraded to a better locking mechanism on my front door, but I supposed even that wasn't completely fool proof in the grand scheme of things.

I began to quicken my pace, already fearing the worst. It was just my luck to have the nice evening dashed by some unfortunate news.

I approached one of the officers, with whom I was familiar, and nervously asked what had happened. Although it was late and dusk had fallen a while ago, the flashing strobe lights from the police vehicles allowed me to see enough of the scene to realise my apartment had been spared this time.

The break-in had happened on the first floor, where nobody currently lived. In front of me, the door to the TV repair shop was gaping open, pieces of shattered glass littering the floor outside.

The officer who I was speaking to asked me how long the shop had been closed, since it was a little grotty looking on the outside, and the windows were caked with dust and cobwebs. I explained that it had been almost two years since the owner - my original landlord - had been admitted to a nursing home and had sadly died. His son had taken over shortly afterwards, but the shop itself hadn't been open for several months. The officer looked uneasy at my explanation and gestured for me to follow him inside the shop. Since it was late, I was the only one around who could really give him any answers, which is why I assumed he wanted to show me around the so-called crime scene.

As expected, the inside of the buildings smelled faintly of damp and there was dust on everything, proving the fact that the place hadn't been open for a while. Other than the musty air and grimy surfaces, the shop was exactly the same as it had been the last time I had visited. There were two sets of footprints in the dust which clearly belonged to the two officers who had first investigated the scene, but other than that, there was no trace of a break-in other than the shattered glass. As far as I could tell, everything that the owner had left behind was still in place, albeit covered in a thick layer of dust. If anyone had been inside, nothing had been disturbed or removed. It all seemed rather odd already, but at that point I didn't know the full story.

The officer continued with his questions by asking me if anything seemed out of place or disturbed, to which I told him that everything had been left where it was, as far as I could remember. This seemed to trouble him even more, and I was beginning to wonder if any *crime* had actually taken place. He then asked if I knew of any other entrances to the shop, other than the front door and the two doors at the rear of the property. As far as I was aware, those three doors were the only way in or out of the shop. There was a door directly in the back, leading to the apartment's stairwell, and another door leading from outside to the basement. Other than that, there was no other way of getting in or out. We checked the other two doors, but when the officer shined his flashlight over them, both were chained shut and padlocked, and the chains were festooned with cobwebs, making it clear nobody had disturbed them in a while either.

When I asked the officer what he thought had happened, he gave me such a clueless look that I was almost caught off guard. Instead of answering me outright, he told me to follow him back to the front door, where the break-in had seemingly happened. He pointed to the broken glass with his flashlight and asked me if anything looked wrong.

After a few minutes of scrutinising the scene, I realised why he had been so doubtful and troubled this whole time.

Judging from the direction the glass had been shattered, and the way it lay on the outside of the building, it was clear that the door had been broken from the *inside* of the shop. When I asked for a possible explanation, he couldn't give me one. Nothing about the scene added up, no matter which way we looked at it. Someone had broken *out* of the shop, not *in*.

"I hate these weird ones," he'd told me after securing the scene with tape and heading back to his vehicle. "I never know how to write them up, you know?"

I have to say, I understood what he meant. There was no probable explanation for why the door had been broken from the inside, especially when the other two doors had clearly been locked and had been that way for a long time. The only explainable was that there had been someone already inside the building, but why had they needed to break *out* if they'd gotten inside in the first place? It didn't make sense, and something about the whole situation made me feel uneasy, like there was something strange about the place I was only just discovering.

The TV repair shop has been completely cleared out now, and is a vacant lot inside the apartment building, but I still get a weird feeling every time I walk past it, especially when it's dark and the shadows play tricks with your eyes. Sometimes, if I'm not paying full attention, it feels like someone might be standing at the empty window, watching me go by. But perhaps that's all just in my head.

JUST A LITTLE HELP

It was late one night, just after 11pm, and I had just finished my shift at the station. The parking lot was empty and quiet, since I'd stayed later than some of the other officers, so I hurried towards my car, bending my head against the wind as it picked up.

As I passed by some of the bushes that edged the parking lot, I thought I glimpsed someone standing there, their silhouette clear against the lights flooding from the building behind me. I turned quickly, my eyes scanning the area, but there was nobody there. I figured I must have been mistaken, but the image was imprinted on my mind, and I could have sworn there had been someone standing right by the shrubbery. Reaching for the flashlight on my belt, I approached the area where I had seen the shadowy figure and shone the light over the ground, searching for any prints. But the soil was dry and didn't hold much in the way of tracks. Beyond the shrubs was an empty field, but there was nobody else in the area as far as I could see, and no evidence anyone had even been there in the first place.

I eventually shrugged it off and headed back to my car, thinking nothing else of it.

A few weeks later, however, I had another experience that reminded me of the figure I'd seen that night. I was working another late shift and I was in the office alone, trying to finish up an incident report. As I was poring over some files at my desk, I felt the air in the room suddenly shift, as though someone had entered, but when I turned to glance back, there was nobody there. I carried on with my work, but a few minutes later I felt a breath on the back of my neck, as though someone had come up behind me and blown against my skin. It wasn't warm, but ice cold, and the shock of it made me leap out of my chair and spin around, scanning the space behind me.

The room was still empty. There was nobody else there apart from me, and I hadn't heard any footsteps of someone entering and leaving. None of the windows were open either, so it couldn't have been a breeze. It definitely felt like someone had breathed on me.

I was already on edge at the point, my heart hammering in my chest, but as I turned back around, I heard a voice whisper "Help me" from somewhere close by. It was female, like a young woman's voice, and there was no possible explanation for it. I was certain the windows were shut, and I was alone on the second floor. But I knew what I had heard.

The whole incident spooked me pretty bad, and I ended up leaving the office and going downstairs to where some of the other officers were still working, so that I wouldn't be alone. I didn't mention it to anyone at the time, not wanting to come across as paranoid, so I tried to forget it and continue with my work.

A few days later, however, I still hadn't forgotten the incident, and I ended up confiding in another co-worker of mine. It had been bothering me a lot, keeping me up at night, so I figured she'd either help me debunk my experiences or figure out the truth. To my surprise, she claimed that she'd experienced some strange things around the station during her night shifts too. And similar to mine, it had begun only a few weeks ago.

She told me that she'd been working a late shift in the office when she thought she'd heard someone walking down the hallway outside, but when she'd checked, there had been nobody there. Another time, she too had seen a shadowy figure who was there one second and gone the next, lingering around the entryway to the police station. Like me, she'd tried not to think too much of it and had brushed it off as simply the result of fatigue. But it was difficult to ignore after confirming we'd both had such similar experiences over the same time frame. There was definitely more to it.

Figuring there was some kind of connection between what we'd seen, the two of us decided to look into recent deaths that had occurred in the local area, wondering if there might be a more paranormal explanation for the events. I'd never given much stock to the existence of ghosts, but at this point, I was beginning to convince myself that there was no other explanation for it. I already knew it wasn't just in my head since there was someone else who could corroborate having the same experiences, and for me, that counted for a lot.

After glancing back over the incident reports for the last few weeks, my co-worker finally pulled out a case that seemed to be a good contender. The only death that had occurred in the last three weeks in the local area was a deadly crash that happened only a few streets away from the station, two and a half weeks prior. A woman had been hit by a drunk driver late one evening, while she was heading home from work. The driver had managed to get away with only minimal scratches, but the woman had been pinned inside her car for almost two hours, suffering blood loss and excruciating pain from her injuries. By the time the paramedics arrived on the scene to extract her, she'd already passed away.

It had been a tragic death, and both my co-worker and I believed this woman was the one who we had seen and heard on several occasions. Maybe she was still hanging around the police station, looking for help after the accident. For all we knew, she might not even realise she was dead, and her connections to the area were keeping her trapped here.

WITHIN THE TREES

Click, click, click

The turn signal continued to flash on the dashboard as I waited at the light for it to turn green. The fact that I was waiting seemed almost foolish. I was sitting there even though not a single car could be seen coming in any direction. Heck, all I'd have to do is flip on the flashers and I could take the left-hand turn, but in all my years of patrol, I'd never used my job for a way to get anywhere quicker. So, there I waited.

Besides, i wasn't in any hurry to get to the next turn on my designated route. Call me superstitious, but I'd never liked driving next to the cemetery, this route especially. There were older stones that had their names nearly worn clean due to age and weather. Once those names were gone, I always wondered if there was anyone left who would remember they even existed or would theirs be a life wiped away by the sands of time.

The red light finally turned to green, and I made my turn. I could already see the lightless stretch ahead of me that was the tell-tale start of the cemetery fence. Even knowing it was coming didn't stop the shudder that passed down my spine.

It's just a coincidence. It has nothing to do with what's up ahead. I wished that was actually the case.

If it were up to me, I would completely avoid

this place, especially at night. But this cemetery had been known to be the location of various illegal activities, (e.g., drugs, drinking, vandalism, etc.), so the three times a night I made my patrol by it was important.

The lights lining the opposite side of the street did little to penetrate the gloom beyond the rot iron fence. I could only make out the first ten to twenty feet, most of which was taken up by a row of maple trees that was supposed to make a person's final resting place more peaceful for the mourners.

I slightly lifted my foot off the gas, and peered into the darkness, hoping to see the same nothing most nights brought. Unfortunately, that wasn't in the cards tonight. Just past halfway I see a shadow moving just behind the trees.

I pull over to the curb and turn my spotlight in their direction hoping to scare them off instead of having to *go* inside. The beam cuts through the night and frames the trespasser. The microphone in my hand freezes halfway up to my mouth as I prepared to tell them to leave.

A black human-shaped figure appeared to be making its way behind the trees. From the distance I was from them I would have been able to clearly make out their features, face included. Instead, all I saw was what appeared to be a black haze. "It" took a few more steps then appeared to turn its head towards me. For a moment we sat there looking at one another before it turned away and walked behind another tree and not reappearing on the other side.

It took me a few seconds to recover my wits. I switched over to the radio and called another unit for backup. In the few minutes that it took for someone to show up I tried to figure out what I was going to say that wouldn't make me sound like I'd lost it. In the end I decided that it made the most sense to tell them I was looking for a trespasser.

As the two of us made our way towards where I had seen the shadow figure, I began looking along the ground for tracks. It was spring and the ground was covered in drops of dew. Every step one of us took left a clear footprint, if someone really was back here, they would do the same.

We arrived at the place behind the trees where I had seen the figure walking and we began looking around, searching for the footprints that would give away the direction they went. Withing a couple of minutes though, the only tracks were the ones we were making ourselves. Whatever I'd seen hadn't left any footprints.

When we got back to our cars, I expected him to give me a hard time about calling him out for nothing. Instead, though he told me that similar things had happened to him when he'd driven by this area too, strange lights, unexplained noises, even seeing figures similar to the one I'd described. Although it did feel good to be believed, the fact that my fears were being confirmed, I'd rather have been called a liar.

LIFELESS FLIGHT

My entire body vibrated along with my jump seat as the helicopter powered its way towards the accident site. If that wasn't bad enough, the engine turning the massive roars that were keeping the aircraft aloft made talking to one another without the headset I was wearing impossible.

"We're about fifteen minutes out." The pilot informed me.

Even without having to rely on roads, the location we were headed made this flight the only chance we had to get the critically injured patient to the hospital in time. Even then, this was likely not going to matter.

A climber had fallen from a height of nearly fifty feet. Details were scarce, but we were told by the dispatcher. "Severe head injury..." was all we knew. What made matters even worse is we would be trying to find a landing zone in a rocky area, plus the sun was just dipping below the horizon reducing visibility and making it more difficult to spot the victim and her friend. Black and whites were on route, but it was likely the injured woman would be dead before they arrived.

I was all keyed up and ready to be there already. I didn't want this to become a DOA. "Come on! Can't this piece of junk go any faster!"

The pilot looked back towards me, I didn't mean for him to hear what I said, but the headset had made him aware of what I was thinking. The look he was giving me told me that he wasn't pleased with my comments on his flying.

"We're going as fast as we can."

"Sorry about that." I wasn't really sorry. "I just hate losing people." This was the only true part of the apology.

"It's fine." From his tone I could tell it wasn't fine, but he turned away from me and focused his attention outside the front window.

Whether he actually sped up or not I couldn't tell but the flight seemed to end quicker than I thought it would. Before long we had located the climbers. Two women stood by a prone figure that lay motionless on the ground.

The third climber complicated matters. It was already going to be a tight fit. If the other climber was also injured trying to work around them was going to be difficult. It was likely that we would have to leave the other two women here and take the fall victim with us.

"I thought there was only two people here." I said to myself.

"What's that?" The pilot said.

"Nothing. Just thinking out loud."

We hit the ground with a solid thud, and I flung the door open and ran in the direction I had seen them standing. He had landed the chopper to a flat area about fifty feet away. I had grabbed the backboard, which I put on the ground next to the woman ready to go to work.

Check for pulse. I couldn't find one.

Check for breathing. Her chest wasn't rising or falling, and I wasn't getting any fogging on the mirror I held in front of her mouth.

"No pulse, no respiration, beginning CPR. You two women, please give us some room.

"I'm the only other person here besides you two ..."

I hadn't really heard what she had said. "We're going to move her to the helicopter. Make sure the two of you don't get in the way. We'll lift on three. One, two, three, lift!"

We moved quickly towards the still open door. I was already going through the list in my head of what we'd do in order to give this woman the best chance to survive. First though I had to make sure the other two were going to be okay until the other units arrived.

"Are you two going to be okay until the other units arrive?"

I already knew she was frustrated by the look she was giving me, but if there was any question, her clipped tone was enough. "I told you, me and her are the only ones here. There is no one else."

I narrowed my eyes at her thinking that this wasn't the time for stupid games. "Look, I saw the other woman here with you when we were landing. Just let me know you're going to be okay until the other units arrive."

She became defiant. "Look, I don't care what you think you saw, but there isn't anyone else here."

I threw my hands up in exasperation. I was wasting time arguing with her and we had a vic what was flat lining behind us. "Fine, whatever. Are {you} going to be okay until the other units arrive?"

Apparently she got the hint that I was done arguing with her. She nodded her accent. "Is she going to be, okay?"

"We'll do the best we can. Now I need you to back away from the craft."

I slid the door shut and immediately felt the ground fall out from under me as the chopper took to the air. Right before I turned to get back to the work of saving the woman's life, I caught sight of the the second woman, who hadn't been there just a second before, standing next to one another. I blinked, just a fraction of a second, and again, the woman was alone.

ROADSIDE MARKER

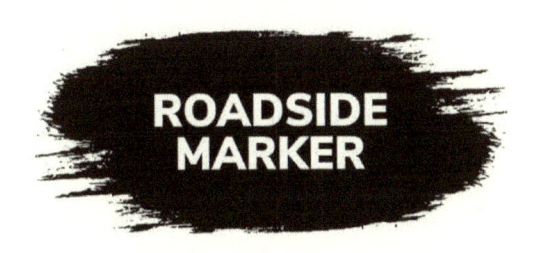

It had been thirty minutes since the last car had passed by me on the stretch of state highway I was watching. Heck, it had been the only vehicle I'd seen in the hour I'd been sitting there. On most nights this was a good place to catch someone going far above the posted limit, but on this night, it seemed particularly deserted.

I tossed the radar gun on the passenger seat, it makes no sense to even hold it up when I'd see a car coming towards me for nearly a mile. There'd be plenty of warning, so why waste the energy? I didn't necessarily want to pull over someone for speeding, or worse DUI, but it was nights like this that seemed to drag on.

Through my left window I see a flash of light. From this distance the two headlights merged together giving it the appearance of a single large bulb coming towards me. As they came closer, they seemed to separate until finally two distinct beams could be seen.

I picked up the radar gun and took the reading. I clocked them at eight miles over the limit. Not enough for a ticket in my estimation, but a warning for sure. Plus, it gave me a chance to break up the monotony.

As they came closer their headlights illuminated the shoulder of the road. I see a dark figure, unmoving, staring towards the ground. It's too far away for me to make out any details, but it is clearly a person.

The dangers of someone in dark clothing on a

state highway at night far outweighs that of a minor traffic violation. The car drives passed me, and I immediately see brake lights as they slow after seeing my patrol car. They're not getting pulled over today, but they don't know that. The taillights aren't nearly as bright, but they do enough to show the silhouette of the cloaked figure, still standing about 100 feet away.

As the car disappears from view so does my dark companion. I turn on my spotlight and swivel it towards where the person was standing. I pass it back and forth along the edge of the road, but I fail to find anything or anyone nearby. I pull out onto the road, hoping to catch whoever had been there a moment ago. The last thing I wanted was to be called back here because of a pedestrian being hit by an oncoming car.

I moved slowly down the road, panning the beam of my spotlight back and forth along the edge and into the brush beyond. Other than the standard weeds and grass I didn't see any sign of the suddenly absent individual.

A shadow moved passed the light. It was too

fast for me to make out what it was, but it seemed to be moving back towards where I had first spotted something. I panned my light over, and sure enough, the dark figure stood.

I couldn't see any face, but he was staring down at some point in the grass, seemingly oblivious to the fact that I had my light trained on him. From where I sat, I could see his shoulders seem to shudder slightly as if he was crying. I reached down and flicked on my flashers and pulled towards him.

For the first time this seemed to get a reaction from him as he turned his head towards me. His face was pale white and where his eyes should be there only appeared to be black holes. The effect was startling and had me pressing myself deeper into the seat.

He turned and started walking away along the side of the road. It wasn't until he reached the edge of the light that I snapped out of it. I moved the handle in order to follow him, but he wasn't there. I jerked the light back and forth, up and down, but there was nobody on the road. Somehow, he had simply vanished.

Curious as to what the person had been looking at, I drove up and parked. I didn't like the idea of exiting my car, fearing the man may reappear, but I had no way of seeing what had caused him such distress without getting out.

I left my door open and the keys in the ignition as I made my way slowly around the edge of the car. Sure, it meant there was a chance someone could take my cruiser, but if the pale-faced man showed up I was going to make a run for it. When I did make it to the other side it didn't take me long to see what was there, a small pink cross had been placed in the dirt.

I'd seen this exact thing many times before. Usually, friends and family placed the memorial to pay tribute to a person who died in an accident at the location. This one being small and pink, I assumed it was a young girl who had been killed here and the man I saw was her father. It was no wonder he was crying.

I made my way back to the car. We didn't have many fatalities in this area, and it wouldn't take much of a search to confirm my suspicions. Within a few minutes I had located the report of a single car wreck that had claimed the lives of two people. I scanned through the text and found that a seven-year-old girl had died in the crash. The next line brought the hair up on the back of my neck, the other victim had been her father.

S.O.S

We were six miles off the coast of Maine, lurching through the swells and troughs as we made our way deeper into the storm. Millions of drops of water slammed against the side of the radio communications shack I was sitting inside of in a seemingly endless torrent of wind and water.

Our Captain had us heading in the direction of an emergency call from a small fishing vessel that had been damaged to do the heavy storm and was quickly taking on large amounts of water. We already knew the ship was going to be a loss, our job was to make sure as many of the six man crew didn't suffer the same fate.

The bow of our ship plunged down the back side of a wave that made it feel as if we were completely vertical only to be lifted back up at an equally leg wrenching angle. Everything that had long since been secured in place, so they weren't flying around the interior. This didn't stop me from hearing everything vibrating in their respected places.

We were moving northeast towards a set of coordinates that had been given to us by the captain of the vessel. When we tried to verify them with Atlantic Command, they told us they had heard no such transmission. It had come in clearly to me, including the name and home birth of from which it came, both of which I had given them and asked for more information on the vessel.

We were coming up on a mile from the

coordinates, still almost 10 minutes before we arrived. I radioed the captain, so he would know our location and what direction we would be approaching him from. his response was panicked, more screaming and begging for help than anything that would tell me that he had received my message. I repeated it again, this time asking him to verify that he had received it.

"Mayday, mayday... this is Vessel ... We have lost power and are ... please help!" The broken message did little to verify that he had heard me.

I scanned the surface of the water as we crested a wave looking for some sign of the other ship. Before I could see anything, we dipped down, stealing my view. Trying to give our position I reached over and began using our signal light in an attempt to establish some sort of communication. About this time, we rose up again, giving me a moment to look out over the water.

By this time I was sure we would have some sort of visual contact if they were still afloat. I tried radioing them again, this time though I didn't get any response, just silence. I feared that we had lost them, but I didn't see any sign that a ship had been here at all.

I was double checking my coordinates that had been given to me when my radio came to life. It was Atlantic Command, not the fishing vessel. They asked me to repeat the name of the ship we had received the communication from and the captain's name. It was an odd request, but I complied with it. Usually, Command gives you some sort of response, but this time nothing came back.

"Do you copy on that information?" I asked after a few seconds.

"Are you sure that is the ship you received the distress call from?" was their response.

At this point in time I was starting to get frustrated with the situation. The other ship still hadn't come into view, and we were right on top of the coordinates where they were supposed to be. Even if they had drifted due to the storm, we would have been able to see them at this point. On top of that I had Atlantic Command asking me to verify information over and over again.

"Yes, I'm sure that is the vessel. Is there a problem?"

A brief pause followed, then finally a response. "From the records we have, that particular ship and everyone aboard was lost at sea."

This seemed obvious, and my response seemed to indicate that. "Yes, they will be if we can't find them. What's your point?"

"No, you don't understand, that ship was lost, six years ago."

I heard the words, but I didn't quite understand what they meant. "Sorry, come back with that last message. Did you say that ship sunk six years ago?"

"Roger, that's what we're saying. Everything we have on it says that the ship and all six crew were lost."

This conversation went on for a few more minutes as we checked to see if there were any other vessels with the same name, but there were none. The only one was the lost ship. Just to make sure we circled around for a while to see if we could find any sign of the missing ship, but in the end, we turned back to port without finding a soul.

When we got back, I pulled the recordings of the radio traffic, hoping to hear the call we had received. During the times when the traffic came in though, all you could hear was my responses. The radio of the other ship was missing.

INSIDE THE CELLBLOCK

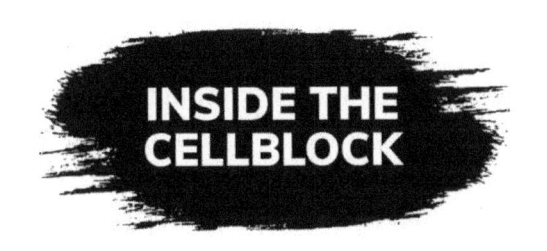

It had only been a few weeks since I had gotten my transfer from the Chicago police department to a smaller, quieter location. After years of discussions, my wife had finally convinced me that it would be better, and safer, if I was working in a place where there wasn't so much violent crime. The dangers of my job, and the stresses that came with it, was taking its toll on our marriage. In the end, a decision had to be made, I applied at a few local precincts, and after a couple months I started working as a jailer.

One of the hardest parts of transferring into a new job is you end up getting one of the less desirable shifts. Right off the gate, I was posted on the overnight crew. I still hadn't gotten used to the late-night hours, especially since most days the place was empty except for the occasional drunk that was pulled off the road.

Most nights I passed the time roaming the two small cellblocks in an attempt to fight off the inevitable drowsiness. This night was no different. I looked over at the clock, 1:24 am, nearly five and a half hours left before I got to go home and get some sleep. There hadn't been a call all night, meaning neither of the other two units had come in to do some paperwork and offer a little company.

Out of nowhere I thought I heard a light rattling noise. The sound was very soft and had ended quickly, enough to have me questioning whether I had heard anything at all. For a moment I held still, even my breath paused in my lungs as I listened for it again.

Seconds passed, yet the air remained devoid of any sound. I had nearly convinced myself that it was just my imagination when it happened again, louder this time.

The noise was coming from one of the cell blocks, but there wasn't anyone housed there. Just the past hour I walked the floor and looked in every cell. Nobody was in them.

I'd heard noises like this before. Drunks would come to and grab the handles to the closed cells and shake them in an attempt to get out only to find they had been locked in. With an empty cellblock though I considered other possibilities water pipes, heating vents, maybe an animal had gotten trapped somewhere... The most likely option was an animal somewhere, since the first two options hadn't happened in the time I had been working there.

I sighed and grabbed my flashlight so I could go and take a look. The rattling noise had become so loud at this point, sounding as if someone was violently shaking the door. My confidence that it was an animal was quickly beginning to fade. My hands shook as I held the key in front of the lock, my courage draining by the second.

I really don't want to go in there... I was a seasoned vet in a city where I took my life into my hands every day, yet I hadn't been more afraid in my life.

The first time I tried to put the key in I missed the hole by almost an inch. Somehow, I manage it on the second try. I turn the key, disengaging the lock. Somehow, as if I have flicked a switch, the rattling comes to a sudden stop.

My mind screams for me to get away, but my body seems frozen in place, my muscles betraying me. I stay that way for almost a minute before I can move again. Much as I want to shut the door, I know I have to go inside.

I push the door revealing the six cells that line the wall to the right. I can't see anyone from outside the door, but my gut tells me that something is *there.*

"Hello?" I call.

Nothing answers me back, but the hairs on the back of my neck stand on end. In my gut I *know* someone, or something is watching me, waiting for a moment of weakness. My eyes automatically find the corners of the room, seeking out a possible source of the discomfort, only to come up empty.

No one is in here, stop acting like a child. What would the other officers say if they saw you like this?

I don't have to answer that question. The shame pushes me into the room. No hidden figure jumps out at me, but the temperature drops significantly, enough that I can now see my breath come out of my mouth in little puffs.

I move quickly, looking in one door after another. The further I go into the tier, the colder it seems to get. By the time I reach the last door, I'm shivering. I briefly turn to look inside and catch a dark form sitting on the bed. I step back to look again, surprised by what the unexpected turn only to find the bed empty.

Standing there, shivering and confused, I feel something touch the back of my neck. The suddenness of it shocks me enough that I make a mad rush for the door. I sprint through, and slam it shut behind me.

By the time I'm able to have a coherent thought, I'm standing at my post, doubled over with my hands on my knees. My mind races, trying to make sense of what has just happened. A loud bang came from behind the door and then quite descended over the jail once more, this time for good.

SNEAK PEAK

ORIGINS
**A HORROR NOVEL
COMING 2022**

ORIGINS
PROLOGUE

Detective Robert Jones watched as the firemen tried to put out the blaze. The air was thick with black smoke, scorching the edges of the building with crippling red burns. The windows had shattered, raining shards of glass onto the hotel's front plaza, more flames licking through the jagged edges with burning ferocity.

The screams had gone quiet a few moments ago. Only the hungry growl and crackle of the flames remained, silencing the cries of those still trapped inside the hotel. Now, the firemen wielded industrial-duty hoses against the raging inferno. The onslaught of water was doing little to quell the fire …

Jones knew it was unlikely anyone had survived. The fire was too intense, too vicious. Nobody was able to get in or out without being consumed by those ravenous flames. Not even the firefighters dispatched to the scene had enough protective equipment to get inside safely.

Beyond the smell of smoke and ash, Jones was certain he could pick up something else; something faintly fragrant and acrid, like the smell of burning flesh or singed hair. He tried not to think about it too much—not when there was so little that he could have done. The firemen had been dispatched as soon as the call came in, but even by then, it was already too late. The fire had already claimed its victims.

"Look at this," Detective Rachel Burke said, drawing his attention away from the blaze. She was kneeling beside a body on the ground, her head cocked as she peered closely at the victim's face. "Look around her mouth."

Jones cleared his throat of smoke and glanced down at the woman sprawled out beside the fountain. The grand feature had been turned off, and the water that pooled at the bottom was cloudy with ash and fallen debris. Somehow, all the luxury and grandeur seemed superfluous against the disaster ongoing around them. The fire, tearing through the hotel without a care for the money and pride that had been thrown into it. Ripped apart in a matter of minutes.

The woman at his feet was young, perhaps mid- to late-twenties, clad in a long gold dress and heels. Her hair was done up in tight blond ringlets and her left arm was thrown out beside her, her fingers reaching toward an empty mug that had somehow survived the fall and remained intact. There were other bodies scattered around the plaza, but they had been victims of the fire, their bodies almost burned to burned beyond recognition? This woman was the only one who seemed to have been killed before the flames reached her.

Her eyes were still open, once a bright blue it seemed, but now clouded over with the veneer of death. Her skin had gone clammy and gray, and Jones thought that something about her seemed almost uncannily vacant, as though she wasn't quite dead, but a puppet waiting for its master.

At his partner's instruction, Jones leaned down to inspect the woman's mouth. Her lips were painted a bright rouge, but they had slackened in death and he could see the foam seeping up between them, as well as the strange discoloration at the corners of her mouth.

"What do you think it is?" he asked, wrinkling his nose at the smell wafting up from her. She couldn't have been dead long, but the throes of decay were already setting in.

Burke's thin eyebrows shot up as she pointed to the victim's mouth, her gloved finger prodding the corner of her lips. "Looks like poisoning to me. See that residue around her mouth? That's common in poison victims," she said, flicking a glance toward the scotch glass. A thin line of red lipstick was smeared around the rim. "We'll have the contents of her drink analyzed. It seems the most likely culprit in administering the poison."

Jones nodded ruminatively. Burke always had an eye for evidence. "What do you think happened here? There's a lot going on, but nobody seems to have any answers." They'd questioned a few witnesses who had managed to escape the fire, but most had no idea what had happened and hadn't seen anyone suspicious in the moments before. It was yet unclear whether it was an accident, or a coordinated attack. All they could do for the moment was use what evidence they had and wait until the hotel was deemed safe to search. Although, it was likely the fire had destroyed any evidence that might have been left inside.

Burke shook her head, pursing her lips. "I can't really say. With the fire and the poison, it seems a lot more happened here than you'd originally think. What about you? Do you have any ideas?"

Detective Jones looked up from the body to the inferno blazing through the hotel. The flames licking the corners of the building seemed somehow alive, and he could feel the hunger and the anger emanating from them. "I can't explain it, but … I don't like the feel of this place."

"How do you mean?"

Jones shifted his feet, lifting a gloved finger to his chin. "I'm not the superstitious type or anything, but something about the place just feels wrong to me. Like all this glamour and luxury is just a façade. It's almost … like this place is cursed."

Burke stared at him in incredulous silence for a minute, before barking out a laugh. "Cursed? Really, Jones?"

The detective shook his head, waving off her apparent amusement. "Yeah, yeah, maybe this heat is making me delirious," he muttered.

Burke sobered. "Maybe. Let's move away from the fire and get someone to collect the body."

Jones nodded in silence as Burke wandered off to find the paramedics, but he stayed where he was, casting an eye over the place.

Despite the humidity of the air against his skin from the fire, a chill touched the back of his neck, running all the way down his spine. Something akin to unease stirred in his chest. The recorded number of accidents that had happened at this hotel couldn't be mere coincidence. Maybe *cursed* wasn't as far off as he'd thought.

Shaking it off, he turned and followed Burke.

ORIGINS
CHAPTER 1

Thomas Hartley tried to be a good husband. He really did.

From the moment he had met Rose, he'd whisked her off her feet and done everything she had wanted, given her everything she had asked for. He had given her the ultimate dream, what she had always desired: a hotel. A place where they could live in solitude in a beautiful building of their own making, earning enough to be comfortable and more.

He'd had the hotel built from scratch, all according to her design plans, the way she had envisioned it for all those years of dreaming. She chose the rooms, the carpets, the furnishings and fixtures, every single painting and sculpture that set the place apart as a high-class luxury. He had sat back and let her do it all, let her thrive in the creative process, making all the decisions. He never said a word of disagreement, never showed his scruples. Never admitted how much he truly detested her taste. But he'd been a good husband. He'd done everything he could to make Rose aware of that fact; to make sure she knew she was one of the lucky ones. The ones who had husbands that would do anything for them. She never had to worry about anything because he would always be there to sort things out when they went wrong. All she had to do was have fun.

Well, now it was his turn.

He wanted to have some fun too.

He'd been a good husband, but now he wanted to play.

Thomas had been what his parents called a "troubled kid."

He'd never been very good at making friends, despite his interest in other children. He was intelligent for his age too, more observant and perceptive than the other kids. Because of that, he'd been a rather lonely child. A lonely child who coveted attention.

He spent a lot of time on his own, out in the woods behind his house.

It was there he had his first brush with death.

He'd been playing among the trees, chasing bugs with a sharpened stick, when he stumbled over something that made a wet, cracking noise when he hit it with his foot. When he peered down, he saw the remains of a fox carcass, half-rotted among the weeds and thistles at his feet. When he'd stepped in it, some of the blood and viscera had leaked out onto his shoe, staining it a gruesome red.

Struck with disgust and a budding curiosity, he used his stick to scrape the mess off his shoe, then used the pointed edge to move some of the fox's loose skin out of the way, exposing its insides. The smell had been rancid, the sight of the organs and the bones gruesome to a child's mind, but it had sparked something in him—some kind of excitement, a curiosity about life and death. Questions about biology and animal physiology plagued him; the way the body worked, ideas of death and mortality.

Death became a fascination for him.

After his encounter with the fox in the woods, his curiosity only grew. He began to purposely go out into the woods in search of more dead things, whether they were fresh or old, the blood still wet and bright or dried to a dark, crusty brown. It didn't matter. The process of decay was a natural part of death, after all.

He played around with death throughout his childhood, his own secret occupation. Nobody else could know the joys of poking, stabbing, dissecting those pitiful little creatures out in the woods. And when he found no more dead ones, he made them himself. He would set traps full of pointy metal teeth and wait for the prey to stumble in them unawares, watching them thrash and squirm helplessly as the teeth bit into them and made them bleed. He was always watching, from the shadows of the trees; watching their struggles grow still, their eyes turn dark and cloudy, their screams dying in their throats. No animal was quite the same. Some of them fought to the very end. Others accepted their fate and succumbed to death quietly. Then they would be his to play with.

Those woods behind his childhood home held a lot of his secrets. All those bones buried deep beneath the soil, his handiwork.

Of course, he'd had to grow up at some point. And as he got older, things changed.

Into early adulthood, he was plagued with voices. Those sinister little whispers in his head, filling his mind with morbid fantasies. Reminding him of the pleasure he'd gotten out in those woods, telling him he needed more, deserved more.

Animals weren't enough anymore. He needed bigger prey. Bigger toys to play with.

So he'd waited. Bided his time. Waiting for the perfect opportunity. All the while, those voices continued to taunt him, to haunt him in the night with fantasies of blood and death, memories of his childhood, when nobody had understood him, when his parents had condemned him for being wrong, for being broken. Disillusioned with life, he'd spent many years learning that people like him didn't have a place amongst normal society. He was an outcast, a reject. But he wanted that to change. He tried to suppress his desires, but that didn't work. Instead, he learned to hide them. He did everything he could to appear *normal*. He was still intelligent, still capable, and it wasn't long before he got a well-paying job and began to integrate properly into the social settings he had been exempt from in his younger years.

And then he met Rose. Naïve little Rose, who had fallen under his spell. He gave her everything she wanted. He gave her the seclusion, the privacy, the luxury that she craved. And in return, he gained her trust, her passion, her desire. And those hidden obsessions began to creep back in, looking for a new outlet. When Rose had proposed building a hotel, in some remote, far-off valley, it had seemed perfect. Everything had aligned as he had desired. He would have the perfect opportunity to satisfy his own cravings, and the perfect façade to hide behind. A future of blood and death, just as he had always wanted.

He'd been a good husband to her. He'd sacrificed years to get to where he was now.

But now it wasn't enough. He was finished with the lies, with the preparation. Now, he was ready.

He wanted more. Needed more. More screams, more blood, more suffering.

He wanted to kill. Dreams and memories weren't enough anymore. He had a craving for blood, for death, and his wife's dream hotel would become the site of his dream, too.

After all, who would miss a lonely traveler, all the way out here?

ORIGINS
CHAPTER 2

Thomas leaned forward slightly over the counter, bridging his fingers together as he flashed a dazzling grin at the young woman standing opposite him. "Your name?" he asked, his voice like silk.

He'd gotten far better at charming people since his lonely childhood years. He'd learned how to attract, to beguile and allure, to throw people off his scent with a smile and a wink, so that they might never suspect the darkness hiding beneath, the fascination with death that he had harbored since he was only a boy.

"Oh, it's Susan Livowitz," she answered in a low southern drawl, shifting her suitcase from one hand to the other as she peered up at him from beneath her lashes.

"Ahh, such a beautiful name," Thomas cooed, his grin widening. In the bright fluorescents above him, his eyes gleamed like emeralds. "Susan…"

With a gloved hand, she tucked a strand of honey hair behind her ear, smiling sheepishly at him. "Thank you."

"How long are you staying?"

"Just a few days."

"I see. Not long at all." Thomas reached behind him and plucked a key from the wall. "I'll put you in Room Five. Is that satisfactory?"

"Yes, that's perfect, thank you," she said, taking the key from him. He reached forward a little more than he needed to, making sure his fingers brushed hers for a fleeting second. Her skin was soft and warm, sending a faint tingle through him.

"Allow me to carry your luggage," he said, stepping out from behind the desk with a slight bow, another charming smile. Appearances were everything in places like these.

"Oh, there's really no need, I can—"

"Please, I insist," he interrupted, taking the bag from her before she could protest further. Now that he was closer, he could smell her perfume, light and fruity, and he dug his teeth into his lip.

His mind was swirling with dangerous thoughts. Uncontrolled desires. He couldn't let her read them on his face.

"Thank you," Susan said, a faint blush appearing on her cheeks.

She's a shy one, he thought as he led the way to her room. *I wonder if she screams with that southern drawl. Or if she's a quiet one. I wonder if her blood is as red as those pouty lips ...*

He schooled his features into a tight smile as she came to walk beside him, running a finger through her hair nervously.

"Are you new to the area?" he asked, keeping his tone polite.

"Yes, I've never been here before. It's rather out of the way. But it's a lovely place."

"Indeed. My wife likes the seclusion of it," he said offhandedly.

"Y-your wife?"

He chuckled lightly, noticing the surprise on her face before she sobered. "Yes, she's the one who runs this place, really."

"I see."

"Although, I hardly see her these days. She's always so busy," he continued with a wink. "It's up to me to entertain our guests."

Another hesitant smile appeared on her lips. Thomas hid a smirk. He would definitely enjoy playing with this one.

"Well, here we are. Room five. Please ring the service bell if you require any further assistance."

"Thank you, sir."

He grinned. "Please, call me Thomas."

"Oh, then, thank you, Thomas."

"Enjoy your stay."

She unlocked the door to her room, casting a furtive glance over her shoulder before dragging her suitcase inside and shutting it behind her.

Thomas's smirk returned, and a tingle of excitement thrummed through his veins like an ember sparkling to life.

She was the one. His next target. She was perfect. Quiet and feminine, not overly confident or brash. Easy to manipulate. The perfect toy.

He would have fun with her, he knew it.

Thomas walked back to the front desk, savoring the excitement he was feeling. His fingers were still hot from the touch of her skin, and he already anticipated what it would be like to feel her bones snap beneath them, her blood spilling over her creamy skin. This was what he had been waiting for. A hotel full of potential suspects, a distraught hotel owner. It was the perfect scenario for him to satisfy his desires without getting caught with blood on his hands.

This wasn't the woods anymore, where he had to hide under the shade of the trees, scavenging for dead things to play with. This was the real world. Full of living puppets.

And it was all his for the taking.

ORIGINS
CHAPTER 3

Rose stood unmoving, her hip resting gently against the chair by the window as she stared straight ahead. Despite the blank look she tried to hold, her thoughts were swirling through her mind.

It had been two weeks since she should have bled. She'd never gone this long before without bleeding, and the consequences were pulling a tight string around her stomach.

Was she pregnant? It was the only possible reason, wasn't it?

"Can you hold still, ma'am?"

A voice drew her out of her thoughts, and she realized she'd let a crack show in her expression. The paint peeked his head over the top of the canvas, a scowl shadowing his brows.

She quickly fixed her expression and straightened, and he dipped back behind it, his paintbrush flicking idly.

Rose fought the urge to roll her eyes. How long did they expect her to stand here, completely still?

Thomas was sitting in the chair next to her, posing with his chin in the air. At least he didn't have to stand the whole time. Rose's ankles were beginning to ache and she struggled to keep her shoulders straight against the urge to slouch.

The portrait had been his idea, of course. He'd been eager to get it completed as soon as possible so that they could hang it over their bed, as though their life was some kind of trophy romance, for everyone to see and admire.

But Rose knew that wasn't the case at all. The reality of their marriage at the moment was far from perfect. She'd noticed that Thomas had become more and more withdrawn over the past few weeks, seemingly without cause. It felt like as each day passed, he pulled further and further away, to the point Rose barely saw him anymore - not in the way she used to. When she woke up in the mornings, he would already be gone, and she barely got more than a glimpse of him throughout the day. He was like a shadow, fleeting and quiet, barely acknowledging her anymore. She would be lucky if they even spoke a few sentences to each other some days.

Is this what marriage is really like? She thought to herself as she shifted her feet, ignoring the scowl of the painter. There was the brief honeymoon phase of love and courting, then life moved on from that whirlwind of romance and became dull. Void of love and passion. Would she be able to rekindle the romance they'd had to begin with, when everything seemed so fresh and exciting? Or was this it now - passing like shadows in the night, barely interacting. What about the baby? Maybe this child would be the key to bringing them closer together again. At least, that's what Rose hoped.

She wanted to believe that her daydreams would become reality, that the baby would bring her and Thomas together again and they would become a growing, happy family, always smiling, always together.

But as things were, it seemed her daydreams would only stay as such. She'd thought that running this hotel together would be their shared dream, their shared passion. But it seemed to have pushed them further apart than brought them closer. And the worst thing was that Rose didn't understand *why*. If there was anything bothering Thomas, he never spoke about it. He rarely divulged his real feelings, and Rose was beginning to get frustrated about the lack of communication between them these days. How could she help if she didn't understand? But every time she asked, he would brush her off, tell her he was busy with the hotel.

"And... done."

The painter's voice brought Rose out of her thoughts, and she looked up, momentarily dazed. She'd been so wrapped up in her own head she'd forgotten where she was.

"Come, take a look," the painted said, waving the brush in his hand as he grinned at them.

Thomas rose stiffly from the chair, stretching his arms over his head, and Rose forced her numb feet to move after him.

Thomas reached the easel first, peering at the portrait with a wide, beaming smile. "Oh, it's divine," he said, nodding approvingly. "Thank you, Jerod." He shook the man's hand vigorously.

Ignoring the pins and needles in her feet, Rose came up behind her husband and peered at the painting. She felt something unfamiliar tug at her chest, and her lips tightened.

Was this really what she looked like? Her eyes… they seemed so sad, so broken. Is this what Jerod saw when he looked at her? People always said that eyes were the doorway to the soul, but she'd never believed it until now. It was almost as though Jerod had seen inside her, seen the inner turmoil and sadness she felt, and painted it upon her face.

She realized, in the growing silence, that Thomas and Jerod were staring at her expectantly, and she quickly regained her composure, forcing a smile.

"It's absolutely lovely," she lied, clasping her hands together.

In reality, she found the painting rather drab. Everything about it seemed… unnatural, from the way they were positioned to the expressions on their face. Thomas's smile seemed forced even on paper, and her eyes were so round and sad. It was like he had painted a shadow of reality, a mere echo. There was no substance here. And she was sure it was because of more than the watery, monochrome color palette.

Thomas shook the painter's hand once more and led him out of the room, speaking idly between them. Rose remained where she was, her lips pursed as she continued to critique the painting.

Maybe it was merely her hormones acting up, but in some sad way, she felt like Jerod had brought her inner struggle to the surface, immortalizing it in this portrait for everyone to see. Rather than filling her with fondness, the painting would only ever remind her of her own helplessness.

She merely hoped that Thomas wouldn't notice the sadness painted on her face when the portrait was hung over their bed.

Please remember to leave a review after reading.

Follow Eve S. Evans on instagram: @eves.evansauthor

or

@foreverhauntedpodcast

Check out our Bone-Chilling Tales to keep you awake segment on youtube for more creepy, narriated and animated haunted stories by Eve S Evans.

Let me know on Instagram that you wrote a review and I'll send you a free copy of one of my other books!

Check out Eve on a weekly basis on one of her many podcasting ventures. Forever Haunted, The Ghosts That Haunt Me with Eve Evans, Bone Chilling Tales To Keep You Awake or A Truly Haunted Podcast. (On all podcasting networks.)

If you love to review books and would like a chance to snatch up one of Eve's ARCs before publication, follow her facebook page:

Eve S. Evans Author

For exclusive deals, ARCs, and giveaways!

ABOUT THE AUTHOR

From the time I was first published to current, (2021) I've learned so much about life and my journey into the paranormal.

I started this journey a few years ago after living in multiple haunted houses. However, it was one house in particular that chewed me up and spit me out you could say.

After residing in that house I wanted answers... needed them. So I began my journey of interviewing multiple people who too have been haunted. Any occuptaion, you name it, I've interviewed them.

What did I learn from my journey so far? I'm honestly not sure if I will ever get the answers I truly desire in this lifetime. However, I am determined not to stop anytime soon. I will keep plugging along, interviewing and ghost hunting. I am determined to find as many answers as I can in this lifetime before it too is my turn to be nothing but a ghost.

I have several books coming out this year and I am very well known for my "real ghost story anthologies", however, these will be mostly fictional haunted house books as I wanted to give myself a new challenge.

If you'd like to read one of my anthologies my reccomedation to start would be: True Ghost Stories of First Responders. In this book I interview police, firemen, 911 dispatchers and more. They share with me some of their creepiest calls that could possibly even be deemed "ghostly."

Also this year I am hoping to get my paranormal memoir out. I want to share my story and journey with everyone. Until then, just know that if you are terrified in your home or thinking you are going crazy with unexplained occurances, you ARE NOT alone. I thought I was going crazy too. But I wasn't.

If you'd like someone to talk to about what is going on in your home but don't know who to turn to, feel free to message me on Instagram or on Facebook.

Forever Haunted Podcast

True Whispers True Crime Podcast

Follow Eve S. Evans on instagram @eves.evansauthor

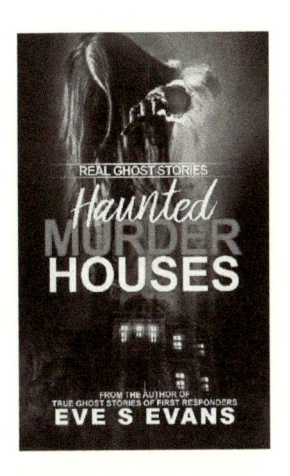

If these walls could talk, they'd tell tales of murder

Are you ready for twisted **true** haunting stories? Haunted houses, whether you love them or hate them, you have to admit there's something creepy about being in a house where a murder has taken place.

What if you didn't know there was a murder in your home until coming face to face with shadow people, demonic entities, apparitions, poltergeists, or creepier beings?

Every single haunted story in this collection will leave you glad you're not the unfortunate soul residing in one of these haunted houses… or are you? Get comfortable, leave the lights on, and enjoy this ghostly collection of stories that will send a chill up your spine no matter how many cups of cocoa you drink.

Don't read these spine-tingling real paranormal stories alone in the dark!

First responders with any real time on the job believe in ghosts. They've experienced events they can't otherwise explain. Same with other professions that deal with injuries, accidents, or death. Police officers, firemen, 911 operators, they've seen the worst that people can do to one another, and they've all had brushes with the unexplained.

Don't believe in ghosts? This book might change your mind steal any hope of sleep.

These stories are unexplainable, true accounts from first responders, police officers, firemen, and 911 operators, told from the perspective of everyday people. Every single tale between these covers is one hundred percent true. Think you can explain them? We dare you to try.

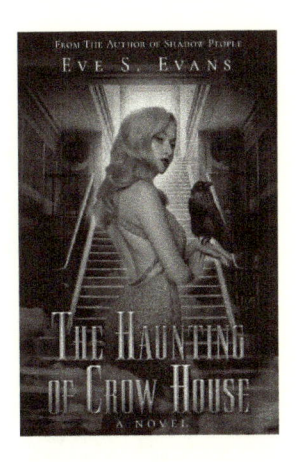

Abigail lost her mother—next she might lose grip on reality...

Still recovering from the loss of her mother after a punishing three-year battle with cancer, Abigail's simply stunned by her new normal. Fumbling through the motions, she learns her mother had secrets when the lawyer informs her of an unknown inheritance— a run-down mansion in the middle of nowhere.

As the only surviving heir; it's her responsibility, her inheritance, though she knew nothing of its existence.

Tired of her day job and hoping this could be a fresh start, she takes a leave of absence to visit the estate. With dreams of converting it into a bed and breakfast, she's excited for the possibilities. Unfortunately, the property is anything but a dream come true; the trouble starts with horrifying nightmares and ends with... well, unexplained paranormal experiences. Only thing is, Abigail doesn't believe in ghosts.

Until she comes face to face with one...

EVE S. EVANS

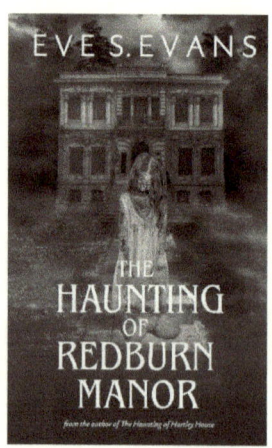

THE HAUNTING OF REDBURN MANOR

from the author of *The Haunting of Hartley House*

They wanted to go viral—now they're just hoping to survive...

Tracking Pure Evil—a podcast dedicated to the spooky things that go bump in the night—have put together a team. A team with one sole purpose; to increase their viewership by staying in the truly terrifying Redburn Manor. With over 200 years of bad luck, death, murder, suicides, accidents and absolute terror, they've found the perfect place… or so they think.

The goal? Going viral, of course.

At first, the place seems harmless; an old house with exaggerated rumors. Until late in the first day of their four-day ghost hunt when something out of the corner of someone's eye sends the group into panic mode. And those disembodied voices; are they ghosts? Or something more sinister? Never mind going viral—will they survive their stay? Or will the house swallow them?

We all wish our pets could stay with us forever... but what happens when they visit us from beyond?
This collection of true paranormal pet stories will have the hair on the back of your neck standing on end. Read accounts from owners who were certain their beloved animals came back from the other side. But don't be fooled; these stories aren't all happy reunions and love.

Some are downright chilling and might make you glad your pet hasn't come back for a visit.

If you think Pet Cemetery is scary; then these spine-tingling true accounts might just keep you awake all night long. Read at your own risk and don't say we didn't warn you.

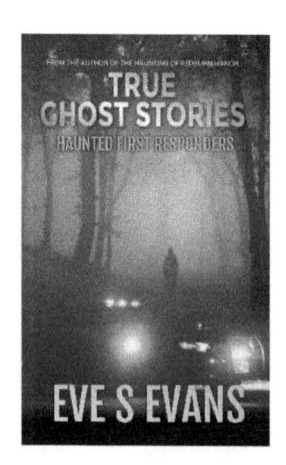

Some of the most haunting unexplained tales from 911 operators, police, firefighters, paramedics and more...

First responders with any real time on the job believe in ghosts. They've experienced events they can't otherwise explain. Same with other professions that deal with injuries, accidents, or death. Police officers, firemen, 911 operators, they've seen the worst that people can do to one another, and they've all had brushes with the unexplained.

Don't believe in ghosts? This book might change your mind steal any hope of sleep.

These stories are unexplainable, true accounts from first responders, police officers, firemen, and 911 operators, told from the perspective of everyday people. Every single tale between these covers is one hundred percent true. Think you can explain them? We dare you to try.

These tales of holiday hauntings will bring a bit of cheer—and fear—to your holiday season!

Are you ready to curl up with some hot cocoa, a warm blanket, and real accounts of spooky holiday hauntings? Then this is the book for you! From poor souls who moved into haunted houses to demonic encounters, poltergeist activity and more, these eerie stories will bring a bit of *boo*! to your merry and bright festivities.

Holidays are a happy time of year, but hauntings don't take the holidays off.

So curl up and dive into these disturbing tales. We recommend leaving the lights on and maybe sleeping with one eye open. After all, these paranormal encounters are all true stories. Enjoy and happy haunted-days.